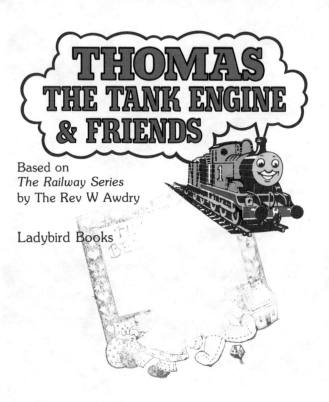

THOMAS THE TANK ENGINE & FRIENDS

Based on
The Railway Series
by The Rev W Awdry

Ladybird Books

Acknowledgment
Photographic stills by Kenny McArthur of Clearwater Features
for Britt Allcroft Ltd.

PERCY
RUNS AWAY

Percy runs away

When Thomas the Tank Engine was given his own branch line there was only Edward who would do the shunting for the big engines.

Edward liked shunting and playing with trucks, but the others would not help him. They said that shunting was not a job for important Tender Engines, it was a job for common Tank Engines.

The Fat Controller was very cross. He kept them in the shed and said that they could only come out when they stopped being naughty. Then he sent for Thomas to come and help Edward to run the line for a few days.

Henry, James and Gordon were in the shed for several days. They were very miserable and longed to be let out. At last, the Fat Controller arrived.

5

"I hope that you are sorry," he said sternly, "and understand that you are not so important after all." He told them that he had a surprise for them!

"We have a new Tank Engine called Percy. He is a smart little green engine, with four wheels. Percy has helped to pull the coaches and Thomas and Edward have worked the main line very nicely, while you have been away."

"But I will let you out now if you promise to be good," he said.

"Yes, sir," said the three engines. "We will."

"That's right," said the Fat Controller. "But please remember that this 'no shunting' nonsense must stop."

The Fat Controller told Thomas, Edward and Percy that they could go and play on the branch line for a few days. They ran off happily to find Annie

and Clarabel at the junction.

Annie and Clarabel were Thomas's two coaches and they were very pleased to see Thomas back again. Edward and Percy played with the trucks.

"Stop! Stop! Stop!" screamed the trucks as they were pushed into their proper sidings. But the two engines laughed and went on shunting until the trucks were in their right places.

Next, Edward took some trucks to the Quarry.

Percy was left alone, but he didn't mind a bit. He liked watching the trains and being cheeky to the other engines.

"Hurry, hurry, hurry," he would call and they got very cross.

After a great deal of shunting on Thomas's branch line, Percy was waiting for the signalman to set the points so that he could get back to the yard. He was eager to work, but he was being rather careless and was not paying attention.

Edward had told Percy about the signals on the main line.

"Be careful on that main line," he warned. "Whistle to the signalman to let him know that you are there."

But Percy forgot all about Edward's warning.

He didn't remember to whistle and the signalman forgot he was there.

Percy waited and waited.

The points were still against him so he couldn't move. Then he looked along the main line.

"Peep! Peep!" he whistled in horror.

"Peep! Peep!" he whistled again, for rushing straight towards him was Gordon with the Express.

Percy's driver turned on full steam and shouted for Percy to go back.

But Percy's wheels wouldn't turn quickly enough and Gordon couldn't stop.

Percy waited for the crash. The driver and fireman jumped out.

"Oo...ooh!" groaned Gordon. "Get out of my way!"

Percy opened his eyes. Gordon had stopped with Percy's buffers just a few inches from his own. But Percy had begun to move.

"I won't stay here. I'll run away!" he puffed.

He went straight through Edward's station and was so frightened that he ran right up Gordon's hill without stopping.

After that he was tired, but he couldn't stop.

Percy had no driver to shut off steam and put on his brakes.

"I shall have to run till my wheels wear out!" panted Percy. "Oh dear! Oh dear! I want to stop! I want to stop!" he puffed.

The man in the signal box saw that Percy was in trouble, so he kindly set the points.

Percy puffed wearily into a nice empty siding.

He was too tired now to care where he went.

"I—want—to—stop!
I—want—to—stop!" he puffed.

"I have stopped! I have stopped!" he said, thankfully.

"Sssh...Sssh!" he gasped as he ended up in a big bank of earth.

"Never mind, Percy," said the workmen as they dug him out. "You shall have a drink and some coal and then you'll feel better."

Gordon had arrived.

"Well done, Percy! You started so quickly that you stopped a nasty accident!"

"I'm sorry I was cheeky," said Percy. "You were clever to stop."

Then Gordon helped to pull Percy out from the bank.

Now Percy helps with the coaches in the yard. He is still cheeky because he is that sort of engine, but he is always *very* careful when he goes on the main line.

THOMAS & THE BREAKDOWN TRAIN

Thomas and the breakdown train

Every day the Fat Controller came to the station to catch his train. He always walked over to have a word with Thomas the Tank Engine.

"Hello, Thomas," he said. "Remember to be patient. You can never be as strong and fast as Gordon, the big blue engine, but you can be a Really Useful Engine. Don't let those trucks tease you."

There were lots of trucks at the station. They were silly and noisy. They talked too much and played tricks on engines that they were not used to.

Thomas worked very hard, pushing and pulling the trucks into place and getting them ready for the big engines to take on long journeys.

There was also a small coach and two strange things that his driver called *cranes*.

"That's the breakdown train," he told

Thomas. "The cranes are for lifting heavy things like engines and coaches and trucks."

One day, Thomas was very busy in the yard. Suddenly, he heard an engine whistling, "Help! Help!" When he looked towards the line he saw a goods train come rushing through, much too fast.

Thomas could see that it was James — and James looked very frightened. He was screaming and whistling. His brake blocks were on fire!

"They're pushing me! They're pushing me!" he panted.

But the trucks were laughing. They were having lots of fun with James. Poor James went faster and faster. He was still whistling and calling for help as he disappeared down the line.

"I'd like to teach those trucks a lesson," said Thomas.

Then came the alarm.

"James is off the line! Fetch the breakdown train – quickly!" shouted one of the men.

Thomas was coupled on to the breakdown train and off they went. Thomas worked his hardest.

"Hurry! Hurry! Hurry!" he puffed.

"Bother those trucks and their tricks. I hope poor James isn't hurt," said Thomas as he hurried along.

They found James at a bend in the line. He was in a field with a cow looking at him. James's driver and the fireman were feeling him all over to see if he was hurt.

"Never mind, James," they said. "It wasn't your fault. It was those wooden brakes they gave you. We always said they were no good."

Thomas pushed the breakdown train alongside James. Then he pulled the unhurt trucks out of the way.

"Oh dear! Oh dear!" they groaned.

"Serves you right. Serves you right," puffed Thomas. He was hard at work puffing backwards and forwards all afternoon.

"This'll teach you a lesson. This'll teach you a lesson," he told the trucks.

They left the broken trucks and then, with two cranes, they put James back on the rails. He tried to move, but he couldn't. So Thomas helped him back to the shed.

The Fat Controller was waiting anxiously for them. He smiled when he saw Thomas.

"Well, Thomas," he said. "I've heard all about it, and I'm very pleased with you. You are a Really Useful Engine!

"James shall have some proper brakes and a new coat of paint," he said. "And Thomas, you shall have a branch line all to yourself!"

"Oh! Thank you, sir!" said Thomas, feeling very proud.

Now Thomas is as happy as can be. He has a branch line and two coaches called Annie and Clarabel. Annie can only take passengers and Clarabel can take passengers, luggage and a guard.

They are both old and need new paint, but Thomas puffs proudly backwards and forwards with them, all day.

He is never lonely. His friends,
Edward and Henry, stop quite often to
tell him the news.

Gordon, the biggest and proudest
engine, is always in a hurry, but he never
forgets to say, "Poop, poop," and Thomas
always whistles, "Peep, peep," in return.